Dangerous Creatures

of the Deserts

Helen Bateman and Jayne Denshire

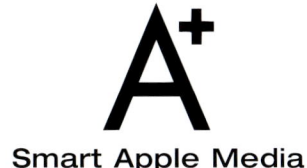

Smart Apple Media

This edition first published in 2005 in the United States of America by Smart Apple Media.

All rights reserved. No part of this book may be reproduced in any form or by any means without written permission from the publisher.

Smart Apple Media
1980 Lookout Drive
North Mankato
Minnesota 56003

First published in 2005 by
MACMILLAN EDUCATION AUSTRALIA PTY LTD
627 Chapel Street, South Yarra 3141

Visit our website at www.macmillan.com.au

Associated companies and representatives throughout the world.

Copyright © Helen Bateman and Jayne Denshire 2005

Library of Congress Cataloging-in-Publication Data

Bateman, Helen.
  Of the deserts / by Helen Bateman and Jayne Denshire.
  p. cm. – (Dangerous creatures)
  Includes index.
  ISBN 1-58340-770-7
  1. Desert animals—Juvenile literature. 2. Dangerous animals—Juvenile literature.
  I. Denshire, Jayne. II. Title.
  QL116.B38 2005
  691.754—dc22

2005042858

Project management by Limelight Press Pty Ltd
Design by Stan Lamond, Lamond Art & Design
Illustrations by Edwina Riddell
Maps by Laurie Whiddon, Map Illustrations. Adapted by Lamond Art & Design
Research by Kate McAllan

Consultant: George McKay PhD, Conservation Biologist

Printed in China

Acknowledgments
The authors and the publisher are grateful to the following for permission to reproduce copyright material:

Cover photograph: western diamondback rattlesnake, courtesy of Karl Lehmann/Lonely Planet Images/Getty Images.

Barry Baker/ANTPhoto.com p. 22; Nigel J. Dennis-Bios/AUSCAPE p. 18–19; Joe McDonald/AUSCAPE pp. 14, 15, 26; APL/Corbis/Tom Brakefield p. 21; APL/Evan Collis p. 23; APL/Corbis/Ralph A. Clevenger p. 9; APL/Corbis/W. Perry Conway p. 16; APL/Corbis/Michael & Patricia Fogden p. 6; APL/Corbis/Patricia Fogden pp. 24, 25; APL/Corbis/Martin Harvey p. 10; APL/Corbis/Philip Marazzi p. 13 (centre left); APL/Corbis/Jose Fusta Raga p. 13 (top); APL/Corbis/Joel Sartore p. 17; APL/Corbis/Paul A. Souders p. 11; Digital Vision Ltd pp. 5, 7; Jiri Lochman/Lochman Transparencies pp. 28, 29; PhotoDisc p. 12; Alain Dragesco-Joffe/Photolibrary.com p. 27; Bartov Eyal/Photolibrary.com p. 8; David Macdonald/Photolibrary.com p. 19 (top); Ben Welsh/Photolibrary.com p. 20.

While every care has been taken to trace and acknowledge copyright, the publisher tenders their apologies for any accidental infringement where copyright has proved untraceable. Where the attempt has been unsuccessful, the publisher welcomes information that would redress the situation.

Please note
At the time of printing, the Internet addresses appearing in this book were correct. Owing to the dynamic nature of the Internet, however, we cannot guarantee that all these addresses will remain correct.

Contents

Life in the deserts	4
Scorpions	6
Fennec foxes	8
Black-backed jackals	10
Camels	12
Gila monsters	14
Western diamondback rattlesnakes	16
Meerkats	18
Harris's hawks	20
Ghost bats	22
Spider-hunting wasps	24
Desert horned vipers	26
Perenties	28
Endangered animals of the deserts	30
Glossary	31
Index	32

When a word is printed in **bold**, you can look up its meaning in the Glossary on page 31.

Life in the deserts

Deserts cover about one-fifth of the land on Earth. There are two types of desert—some are hot and dry, others are cold. In hot and dry deserts, the temperature ranges from 50°F (10°C) in winter to 131°F (55°C) in summer. In cold deserts, the temperature ranges from -40°F (-40°C) when snow covers the ground in winter to 113°F (45°C) in summer. However, a region is not a desert because of its temperature, but because of its dryness. If an area gets less than 10 inches (25 cm) of rain each year it is known as a desert.

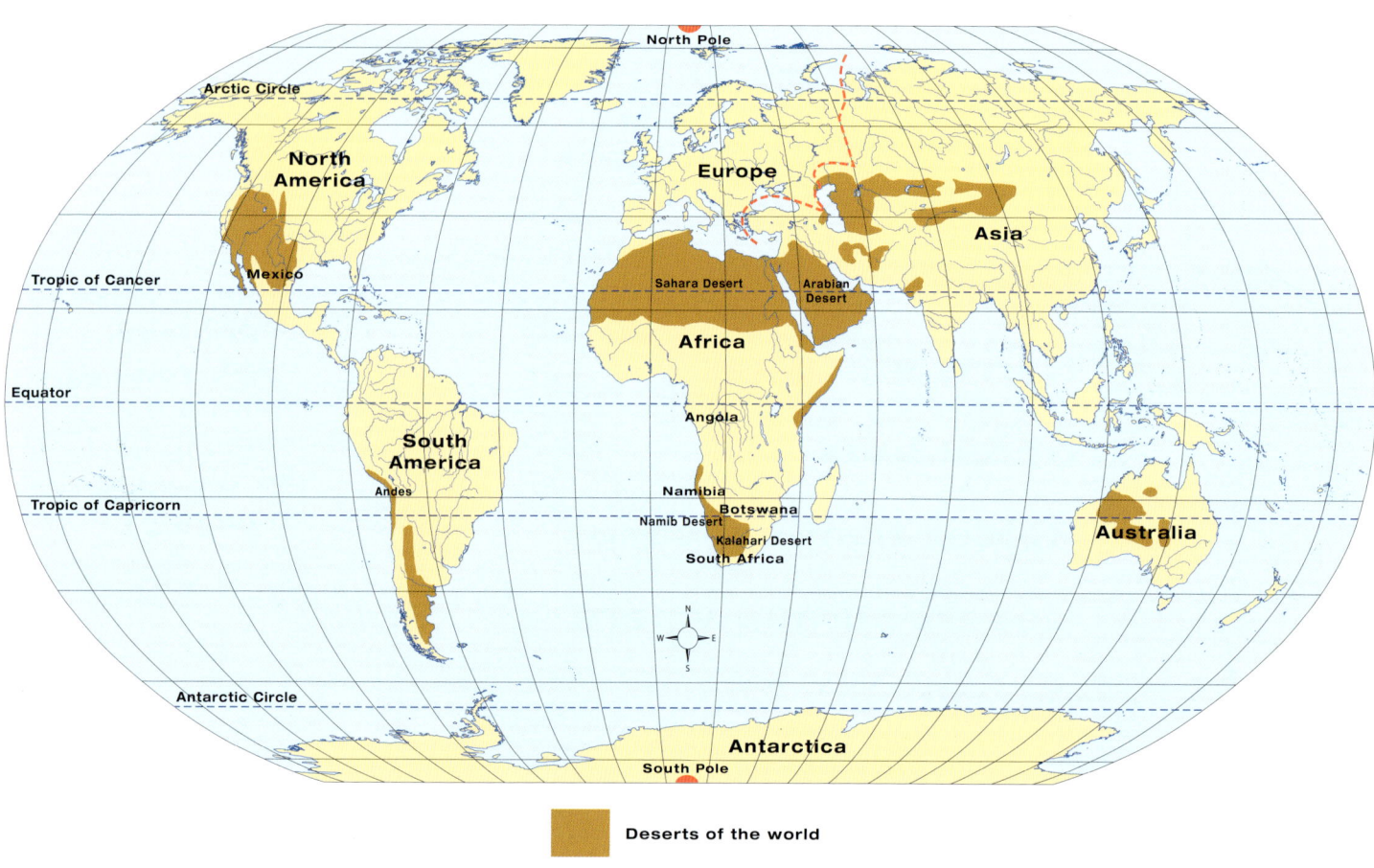

▲ There are deserts all over the world. Those that are closest to the equator are hot and dry deserts. Those that are closer to the North and South poles are cold deserts.

▲ Deserts can be wild, barren, and dangerous. They are home to thousands of creatures.

▲ The desert food chain has four links or levels. The animals from each level survive by eating something from the level below.

Danger and survival

Animals living in deserts behave dangerously because they need to survive in their **habitat**. All creatures have to find food and shelter and often need to defend themselves against other animals at the same time. For many creatures, it is a case of kill or be killed.

Some desert creatures live on plants, but most have to hunt and eat other animals to survive. Some creatures of the deserts are dangerous to humans, but usually only if they feel threatened by them.

The natural **food chain** of the deserts begins with plants and shrubs. These are eaten by animals such as rats, insects, and lizards, which all belong to the second level of the chain. The next level are those animals, such as snakes and scorpions, that eat the plant-eaters. On the highest level of the food chain are the top **predators** of the deserts, such as hawks and foxes.

Scorpions

VITAL STATISTICS
LENGTH
from 0.2 inches (4 mm) to nine inches (23 cm)
WHERE FOUND
worldwide in warm climates

Scorpions are the oldest member of the spider family. They are aggressive creatures, and all species are poisonous. Most are not dangerous to humans, but there are a few species that can kill an adult in minutes.

There are 1,500 species of scorpion living all around the world. They are especially suited to living in hot, dry deserts because their body has a tough covering like a shell, which stops them from losing moisture. They have a head like a spider's and their body is divided into 12 sections. The last five of these sections make up what people call their "tail."

fact flash
Some scorpions can go for a year without food.

▼ When scorpions are born they climb onto their mother's back for protection. They stay there for the first week or two of their life.

Night hunters

Scorpions hunt mostly at night. They stay out of the heat in the daytime, sometimes burrowing as far as seven feet (2 m) under the surface to keep cool. Although scorpions have 12 eyes, they do not see very well. In fact, some species are blind. Their legs and body are covered in hairs and small **organs** that help them to find their **prey** by sensing any **vibrations** nearby.

Scorpions often use the **venom** in their sting to defend themselves from their predators, such as bats, owls, and snakes.

▲ A scorpion's venom is stored in a "bulb" just near the end of its tail. The scorpion poisons its victim through the sharp, curved stinger.

All in the family

Scorpions hunt insects and spiders and even other scorpions. A few of the larger scorpions are able to overpower lizards and mice. They grab their prey with their huge **pincers** and tear it apart. If the animal is too big to hold with their pincers, scorpions swing their poisonous tail over it and sting it. Once the prey becomes paralyzed, scorpions inject a fluid into their victim to help break down its tissue and turn it to mush. This makes the prey easier to eat. This whole process can take hours.

DANGER REPORT

In March 2003, a 70-year-old man was stung several times by a scorpion. This attack was unusual because the man was in a plane at the time. As the plane was coming in to land, the man felt something crawling on his back, stinging him several times. He had been visiting relatives in the Mexican countryside and the scorpion had hidden in his clothing. The man was rushed to hospital and luckily, was saved.

Fennec foxes

VITAL STATISTICS

LENGTH
up to 24 inches (60 cm) (including tail)

WEIGHT
up to three pounds (1.5 kg)

WHERE FOUND
Sahara Desert, northern Africa and the Arabian Desert

Fennec foxes are the smallest foxes in the world, but this does not stop them from being very capable hunters. They are cautious near humans and are not likely to be dangerous to them, but they are deadly to their natural prey.

Fennec foxes are very social animals. When they find a mate, they stay with it as a pair for the rest of their life. They live underground, and each fox digs a **den** for itself. They often dig their dens close to one another. Sometimes up to 15 foxes live in the same area.

▶ Fennec foxes have ears that are up to six inches (15 cm) long. They help them to hear prey.

fact flash
Fennec foxes pant very quickly, up to 690 times a minute, and this helps them to stay cool.

Built for survival
Fennec foxes can survive for a long time without water. They hunt at night, when the desert is cool. Their thick body fur protects them from the cold. They have such good hearing they can even hear large insects walking on the sand or calling to each other.

Varied diet
Fennec foxes hunt insects, lizards, snakes, and small **rodents**. Their large ears act like funnels, sending sound down to their eardrums and helping them to detect prey. They turn their ears and their head in all directions to pinpoint exactly where a sound is coming from. When they do detect their victim, they move fast. Their long, bushy tail helps them to change direction in the chase. They spring onto the creature, pin it down with their front feet, and then seize it in their teeth. They chew their prey, breaking it apart before swallowing it.

fact flash
Fennec foxes curl their tongue while they pant so that none of their spit drips off and is wasted.

◀ Fennec foxes have light, sand-colored fur, which reflects the sun's heat and helps them blend in to the desert landscape.

Black-backed jackals

VITAL STATISTICS
LENGTH
four feet (1.3 m) (including tail)
WEIGHT
up to 33 pounds (15 kg)
WHERE FOUND
eastern and southern Africa (Namib and Kalahari deserts)

Black-backed jackals are cunning predators, but they are not dangerous to humans. They are members of the dog family. They have reddish brown fur with a distinguishing strip of black and white hair that runs from their head to the tip of their tail.

Black-backed jackals form long-term relationships and live with the same mate for many years. The young stay with the family, learning how to hunt and how to raise pups before they go off to find their own mates. Black-backed jackals form family packs to defend their territory against their predators.

Hunters in hiding

Black-backed jackals usually spend their day hidden in the bush, coming out to hunt at night. They often work together, hunting in pairs or in packs. That way they can attack much larger animals, such as young lion cubs, impala, and young wildebeest. When they hunt alone, they are more likely to choose smaller prey, such as rodents, lizards, snakes, birds, and insects.

▲ Black-backed jackals will eat just about anything that moves. They are not very fussy about their prey. They will hunt whatever is available.

fact flash

A female jackal moves her pups every few days so predators will not find them.

fact flash

Jackals sometimes have to fight other scavengers, such as hyenas and vultures, for the right to eat a carcass.

Last resort

Black-backed jackals are very successful hunters, but they will resort to eating fruit, or to **scavenging**, if live prey is not available. Black-backed jackals have even been known to help other animals, such as lions or cheetahs, to find and kill prey just so they can eat the remains of the victim afterwards. This is a dangerous way to get a meal, however, because other dangerous animals may be attracted to a **carcass**.

▼ Black-backed jackals can sense when their prey is young, sick or weak. They separate it from its pack and move in for the kill.

Camels

VITAL STATISTICS
LENGTH
up to 11 feet (3.4 m)
WEIGHT
up to 1,521 pounds (690 kg)
WHERE FOUND
Dromedary—North and East Africa, West and South Asia. Introduced to Australia.
Bactrian—eastern Asia

▼ Dromedary camels have been used for transportation as well as their fur, meat, and milk for thousands of years.

Camels are **herbivores**, so they do not hunt and eat other animals. However, they are dangerous to humans and other animals because they are so large and aggressive.

fact flash
When camels run, they sometimes lift all four feet off the ground at the same time.

There are two types of camel. Dromedary camels, which have one hump, make up about 90 percent of the world's camels. These camels live in the desert, but they have been **domesticated**, or tamed, and are now almost **extinct** in the wild. Bactrian camels, which have two humps, make up the rest of the world's camels. There are now only a small number of them.

Big, mean, and nasty
Wild camels are safe from most predators because of their size and aggressive nature. They live in small herds of one male with a group of females and their young. The male keeps other males away from the group.

Camels store fat in their hump and use it as a source of energy when food is scarce. They can go without drinking water for up to two months. When they do finally reach water, camels can drink as much as 190 pints (90 l) in 10 minutes.

12

▲ Camels have fatty pads under each of their toes to help spread their weight out so they do not sink into the sand.

▲ Camels have very large teeth. These can inflict serious wounds, which can easily become infected.

Killer camels

Domesticated camels have killed a number of people. They spit, kick, and fight. They can kick forward and backward, and even when they are sitting down, they can still kick sideways.

Male camels are especially dangerous to other males during the breeding season. They become very aggressive and fight each other to try to take over a herd.

DANGER REPORT

On December 13, 2003, a 48-year-old man received a fractured skull when a domesticated camel picked him up by his head. As the camel's mouth clamped onto the man's head, it fractured both sides of his skull. Surgeons repaired the man's skull by inserting a metal plate into his head. The man recovered, but suffered minor brain damage.

Gila monsters

VITAL STATISTICS

LENGTH
20 inches (50 cm)

WEIGHT
up to three pounds (1.35 kg)

WHERE FOUND
southwest North America, northern Mexico

Gila monsters are one of only two venomous lizards in the world. Although they are shy creatures, gila monsters will bite viciously when they are threatened. They have a large, heavy body with short legs, a huge head, and small eyes. Their body has pink, orange, and red markings, and they have a black face.

Gila monsters spend much of their life underground in the bushier parts of a desert. Sometimes they steal the burrows of other animals and sometimes they dig their own with their sharp, curved claws. They are slow movers, so they prefer to lie in wait and **ambush** their prey rather than chase it.

fact flash

Gila monsters fight each other in the mating season. They bite each other, but they are not affected by the venom.

Mighty bite

Gila monsters have strong, powerful jaws and their sharp teeth can do a lot of damage. They are dangerous to humans, but rarely kill them. When gila monsters bite, they clamp on so tightly that sometimes humans have to force a stick into their jaws to make them release their grip.

◀ When gila monsters are in danger, they defend themselves by hissing loudly at their predators.

▶ Gila monsters eat a wide range of small prey, but one of their favorite meals is birds' eggs.

Seasonal hunting

Gila monsters hunt at night in summer and during the day in spring and fall. They **hibernate** in winter. Gila monsters eat eggs, and hunt rats, rabbits, small birds, frogs, and other lizards. They use their tongue to detect their prey, flicking it out in front of them to pick up scents as they crawl along. Most of their prey is small, so they do not always have to use their venom. It comes in handy if there is a struggle.

Venom

Gila monsters' venom is produced by glands in their jaw. It runs down specially grooved teeth and is chewed into the victim by the lizard. This venom can paralyze smaller animals and stop their heart. Although it is as poisonous as the venom of a western diamondback rattlesnake, it is injected in such small amounts that it is rarely fatal for a human. There is no **antivenin** available.

fact flash

In winter, gila monsters can live for months off the fat that is stored in their tail.

15

Western diamondback rattlesnakes

VITAL STATISTICS
LENGTH
up to seven feet (2 m)
WHERE FOUND
southern North America and northern Mexico

Of all the rattlesnakes in the United States, the western diamondback kills the most people. These rattlesnakes live in a number of areas, but are very much at home in desert environments. They are large, heavy, and poisonous. Their back is covered with dark, diamond-shaped blotches, which are a good **camouflage** for life in scrubby, rocky areas.

Spring danger

Western diamondback rattlesnakes are at their most dangerous in Spring, just after they have finished hibernating. This is when they are hungry and also when they are looking for a mate. They are not aggressive unless they are disturbed or threatened. They sound their rattle as a warning, and if they are given room, they will usually retreat. The bite from their **fangs** is very painful and the venom, which breaks down blood cells, can cause the death of a human adult within an hour or two.

▲ The fangs of a western diamondback rattlesnake are special teeth with tubes inside that deliver the venom. The snake has six more fangs on each side of its face ready to be used if necessary.

DANGER REPORT

In March, 2004, a U.S. veterinary surgeon had a lucky escape when he was bitten on the thumb by a western diamondback rattlesnake that had been brought to his surgery. He was taken first to a medical center, then to a hospital, neither of which had the antivenin to save him. Eventually, antivenin was found in another city and was rushed to the man's aid. Doctors said that if it had taken even 30 minutes longer the antivenin would have been useless to him.

▼ Western diamondback rattlesnakes rear up as they rattle to look threatening, and as a warning. If this warning does not work, they may strike.

fact flash

Baby rattlesnakes are not born with a rattle. They get their first one, called the button, after they have shed their first skin at about two weeks of age.

On the hunt

Western diamondback rattlesnakes usually hunt at night, sensing the body heat of their prey. Their prey is rabbits, squirrels, prairie dogs, rats, and lizards. They ambush victims near rocks or in grass, or attack them in their burrows. Sometimes they strike an animal that is heavier and wider than they are and then swallow it whole, and headfirst.

▶ A rattlesnake's rattle is hollow. It is made of a material like human fingernails. A new section is added every time the snake sheds its skin. This means that the louder the rattle, the bigger the snake.

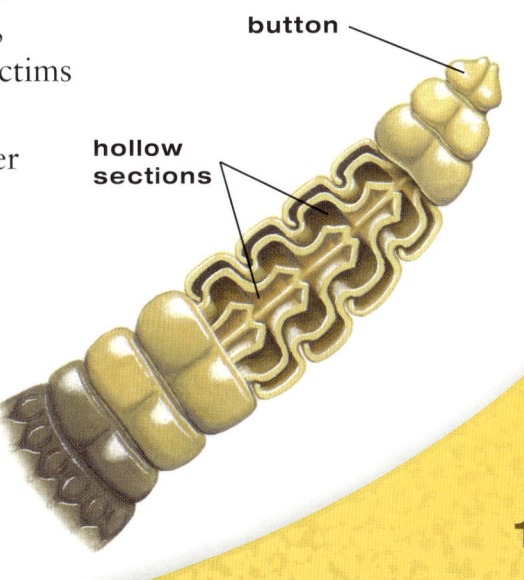

17

Meerkats

VITAL STATISTICS
LENGTH
22 inches (56 cm) (including tail)
WEIGHT
34 ounches (964 g)
WHERE FOUND
Angola, Botswana, Namibia, South Africa

Meerkats belong to the mongoose family. They are quick and successful hunters, but they are not dangerous to humans. They have a long, low body, short legs, and long, sharp claws that they use to dig their burrows. They have a gray coat, with darker stripes across their back and tail. They have dark rings under their eyes that make them look bigger. This tricks other animals into thinking meerkats are larger than they really are.

▶ Meerkats on guard duty keep making soft sounds to let the rest of the group know everything is all right. If a predator comes near, the sound they make changes first to a beep and then to a cry depending on who, and how close, the predator is.

fact flash

Meerkats close their ears when they burrow underground to prevent dirt from getting in.

18

fact flash

Meerkats use more than 20 different sounds to communicate with each other when they are feeding, grooming, playing, and on guard duty.

▶ Meerkats eat a varied diet, but one of their favourite meals is a scorpion.

Hunting

Meerkats hunt beetles, grubs, lizards, snakes, and small rodents. They have very good long-distance sight, but they often miss prey that is right in front of them. This is why they often depend on their sense of smell to find food. When meerkats do find their prey, they quickly attack and devour it. They like to hunt scorpions, but they first bite off the poisonous stinger before they start to eat the rest. Meerkats seem to be **immune** to scorpions' venom.

Underground homes

Meerkats live beneath the ground in tunnels at night and come out to hunt during the day. Sometimes they allow other animals to share their burrows, but they never share with any animal they think is likely to steal their food.

Meerkats live together in packs. Sometimes rival packs of meerkats fight over their territory and kill each other. Within a pack, each meerkat has a special job to do. Some take care of the pups, others search for food and teach the young ones how to hunt, while still others stand guard for predators such as eagles. When a predator comes near, the guard sounds the alarm and all the meerkats go running for the safety of their burrows.

Harris's hawks

VITAL STATISTICS
LENGTH
34 inches (86 cm) (including tail)
WIDTH
four feet (1.2 m) (wingspan)
WHERE FOUND
southern North America, Mexico and South America east of the Andes

Harris's hawks are fierce hunters of a wide range of prey, but they are not dangerous to humans. They live in a number of different habitats, one of which is desert scrubland. They survive easily in hot, dry areas where water is scarce because they get moisture from the animals they eat.

Harris's hawks are **raptors**, or large birds of prey, with reddish brown and black feathers, a yellow, hooked beak, and yellow feet. They have large wings, which they often spread over their catch, to hide it from other birds. They have very sharp eyesight, which is many times better than a human's.

Group living

Harris's hawks live in groups. The young stay with their parents for some time to help them hunt, and to help their parents raise the next chicks. They also hunt in groups, cooperating with each other to catch their prey. This allows the hawks to go after much larger prey than if they were attacking on their own. It also means that all the birds get more to eat, and the young birds get extra training in hunting.

◄ Harris's hawks build their nests high on the top of cactus or tall yucca plants, out of the way of predators.

20

fact flash

When there are no places to rest, Harris's hawks stand on each other's back, sometimes three birds high.

Wide variety

Harris's hawks hunt insects, lizards, birds, and **mammal**s, such as rats and jackrabbits. They hunt in groups of up to six birds, taking turns as leader in a chase to make sure they exhaust the animal but not themselves. Sometimes they attack as a group from several directions to panic an animal into running into open ground. Once the animal is out of hiding, one of the hawks herds it toward the rest of the group. When the prey has been caught, the members of the group share their kill.

▲ **Harris's hawks fly low and fast to catch their prey.**

Ghost bats

VITAL STATISTICS
LENGTH
up to six inches (15 cm)
WEIGHT
six ounces (165 g)
WHERE FOUND
Northern Australia

▼ Ghost bats are strong. They can easily carry large prey.

Ghost bats are swift, efficient predators but they are very shy creatures that avoid contact with humans, and are not dangerous to them. Ghost bats are the only **carnivorous** bats in Australia. Their wings are almost see-through, and their pale, almost white color gives them their name. Their body is covered in fur and they have large, sensitive ears that help them to hear their prey. Female ghost bats have one baby each year.

fact flash
Ghost bats are the only bats that eat animals other than insects.

Safety in numbers

In the daytime, ghost bats live in **colonies**, usually in caves, but at night, they hunt alone. They are skilled hunters that can catch animals in the air or on the ground. They can even pick frogs out of the water. As well as large insects, ghost bats catch lizards, birds, frogs, small mammals such as mice, and other, smaller, insect-eating bats.

Finding prey

Ghost bats use their large eyes as well as **echolocation** to find their prey. They swoop on the animal quickly, and when they reach it, they fold their wings around it and kill it with powerful bites. They fly off with their victim to a favorite cave or rock shelter—a special feeding place that they use over and over again.

Ghost bats rip the meat off the prey with their sharp teeth. They eat small feathers, fur, and some bones, but they drop the larger bones and feathers to the ground.

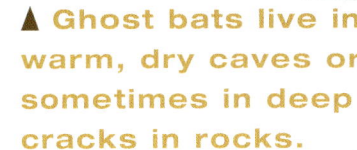
▲ Ghost bats live in warm, dry caves or sometimes in deep cracks in rocks.

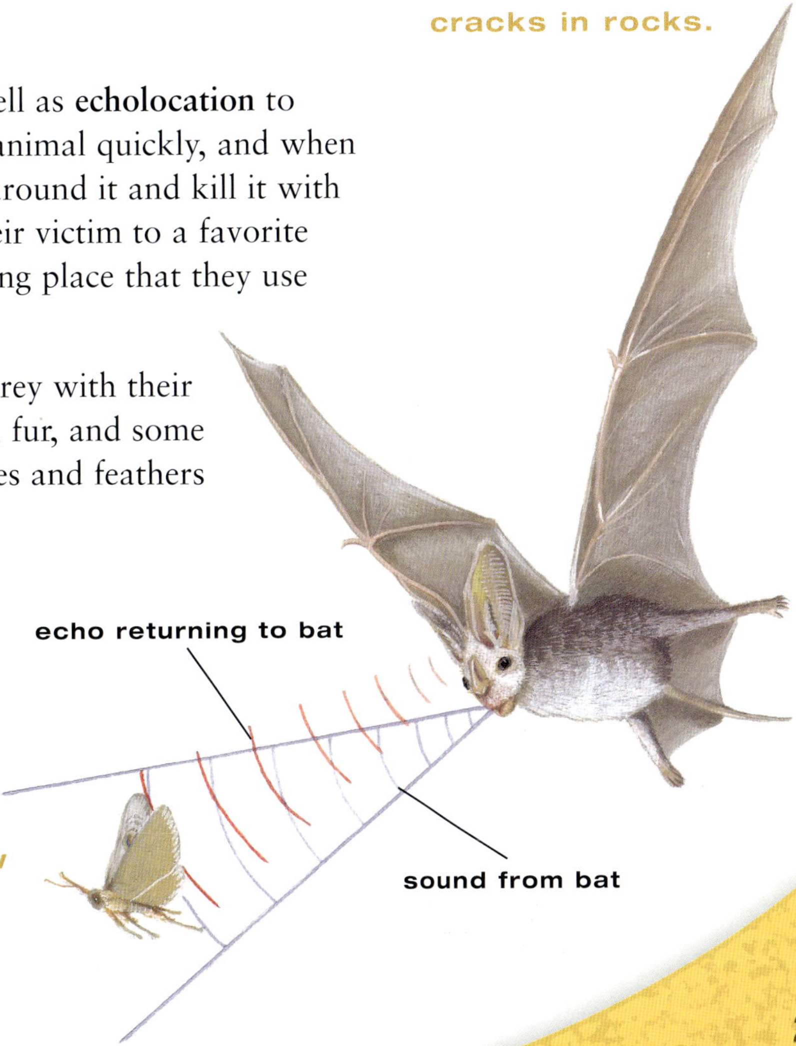

▶ Ghost bats find their prey by echolocation. They make squeaks and listen for their echoes. The bats can tell how close the prey is by how quickly the echo returns to them. The faster the echo, the closer the prey.

echo returning to bat
sound from bat

23

Spider-hunting wasps

VITAL STATISTICS
LENGTH
up to three inches (8 cm)
WINGSPAN
up to six inches (15 cm)
WHERE FOUND
worldwide in warm climates

Spider-hunting wasps are deadly to spiders but are not especially aggressive to humans. There are many species of wasp that hunt spiders throughout the world, especially in desert regions. One of the best known groups is the tarantula hawk wasp, which is the largest of the spider-eaters. Although tarantula hawk wasps are not dangerous to humans, their sting is considered to be the most painful of any North American insect. Their orange wings warn other animals to stay away.

fact flash
Tarantula hawk wasps have a sting that is as painful as an electric shock.

Sun lovers

Spider-hunting wasps are most active in summer during the daytime, although they do try to avoid very high temperatures. Much of the time they feed on the nectar of flowers, but when it comes time for the female to lay her eggs, she becomes a fierce hunter. The female's task is to find a spider that will provide a breeding place for her young. Once she finds the spider, she paralyzes it and stores it in a burrow. Then she lays an egg on it. When the egg hatches, the newly born wasp grub feeds hungrily on the paralyzed spider.

▼ A spider-hunting wasp sometimes digs a hole in which to bury its paralyzed victim.

24

▼ A female tarantula hawk wasp has to sting a spider before it bites and eats her. The battle between a tarantula hawk wasp and its prey can last for hours.

Scratch and attack

Spider-hunting wasps disturb the front of the spider's nest and attack it when it comes out. If that does not work, they dig down into the burrow to catch the spider.

Some spider-hunting wasps dig their own hole and carry their paralyzed prey to it before laying an egg. Other wasps leave the paralyzed spider in its own nest and lay an egg on it there.

fact flash

The female tarantula hawk wasp is the world's largest wasp.

Desert horned vipers

VITAL STATISTICS
LENGTH
24 inches (60 cm)
WHERE FOUND
North Africa

Desert horned vipers are found in the Sahara Desert, North Africa. They are extremely venomous snakes, but they are not aggressive to humans.

Desert horned vipers are a tan color, with darker spots down the back. This coloring helps to camouflage them against sand or rocky ground. Their broad, triangle-shaped head has two horns that stick out above each eye. These horns may help to protect their eyes from injury.

Danger signal

Desert horned vipers have very rough scales, which they rub together when they are threatened. This produces a rattling sound, which frightens off their predators. In the hottest part of the day, desert horned vipers bury themselves almost completely in the sand. If there is no sand, they hide under a rock or in the burrow of another animal. Desert horned vipers usually hunt during the night.

▲ Desert horned vipers bury themselves in the sand to stay cooler, but they keep their eyes above ground so that they can keep watch.

▲ The desert horned viper's fangs fold back when its mouth is closed.

◀ When it is about to strike, the snake opens its mouth wide. The fangs pop down ready to inject venom.

26

fact flash

Desert horned vipers move by twisting themselves sideways. They can travel at about two miles (3 km) an hour.

Sneak attack

Desert horned vipers hunt birds, lizards, and small mammals such as rats. They lie in wait, half-buried until a lizard or rat comes within reach, and then strike them quickly with their fangs. Their venom paralyzes the prey, breaking down its blood cells. As a result, the prey bleeds internally and dies.

▼ Desert horned vipers have rough scales that help them keep a grip on the sand. This makes it easier for them to move through the sand.

Perenties

VITAL STATISTICS
LENGTH
up to eight feet
(2.5 m)
WEIGHT
up to 33 pounds
(15 kg)
WHERE FOUND
Western and Central Australia

Perenties are ferocious hunters, but they are shy with humans and attack only when threatened. A human bitten by a perentie will most likely develop a severe bacterial infection.

Perenties are the largest **monitor** lizards in Australia, and the second largest in the world. Their body is brown or black with large, yellow or cream spots on the back and tail. They have a large head, sharp claws and teeth, and a long, strong tail.

DANGER REPORT

Perenties are not usually aggressive to humans but they will react by biting and scratching if touched. Their powerful tail can also be dangerous to people. Perenties have been known to mistake people or horses for trees, climbing up them to try to escape. In 1994, a perentie climbed and severely bit a professor with a scientific group of people in the Great Victoria Desert, Western Australia.

fact flash

Perenties can kill kangaroos. They pull apart the ones that are too large to be swallowed whole.

Hiding for comfort

Perenties stay out of the extreme heat by digging burrows or hiding in deep rock crevices. They come out of these to hunt, often traveling a long way in search of prey. They hibernate in winter.

Perenties are fast runners. They run swiftly on all four legs, or sometimes on just two legs for short distances. If they are threatened, they puff up their throat, hiss, and strike at their opponents with their muscular tail. Perenties will also lunge forward with an open mouth, either in defense or attack.

▲ During the breeding season, male perenties fight each other over the females.

Part-time scavengers

Perenties sometimes scavenge, but mostly they track live prey, usually by sight. When they catch their prey, they kill it by shaking it violently. Perenties eat small mammals, other lizards, snakes (even venomous ones), insects, and birds.

◀ Perenties eat their small prey whole. They pull apart larger prey with their powerful arms and claws.

Endangered animals of the deserts

More than 5,000 animal species in the world today are endangered. They are in danger from their competitors and predators, and they are in danger from natural disasters, such as droughts, floods, and fires.

But the greatest threat to animals comes from the most dangerous animals of all—humans. As more and more people fill the Earth, there is less room for wildlife. Humans clear land to put up buildings. They farm land for crops or grazing, or they mine it to produce fuel. Precious wildlife habitats are destroyed.

Here are just some of the animals that are in danger of vanishing forever from the deserts of this planet.

ENDANGERED ANIMAL	WHERE FOUND
African wild ass	Eastern Africa
Bactrian camel	Eastern Asia
Bilby	Australia
Desert bandicoot	Australia
Desert monitor lizard	Australia
Desert rat kangaroo	Australia
Gila monster	Southwest North America and northern Mexico
Large desert marsupial mouse	South Australia and Western Australia
Mexican bobcat	Central Mexico
Sand gazelle	Middle East

You can find out more about saving the world's wildlife by visiting the World Wildlife Fund (WWF) at http://www.panda.org.

Glossary

ambush to attack after waiting in a hiding place

antivenin the medicine given to someone bitten by a venomous animal to stop the venom from hurting them

camouflage something in an animal's appearance that helps it to blend into the background

carcass the dead body of an animal

carnivorous meat-eating

colonies groups of animals that live close together

den an animal's burrow or shelter

domesticated tamed and trained to live with people

echolocation a system used by some animals, such as bats, of finding their way around by using sound rather than sight or touch

extinct no longer existing

fangs long, sharp, hollow teeth that are used by snakes to inject venom

food chain the relationship between living things. It shows which animals eat which in order to survive

habitat an animal's natural living place

herbivores animals that eat only plants

hibernate to completely rest during winter, often underground

immune not able to be affected by a poison

mammals animals whose young feed on their mother's milk

monitor a type of very large lizard

organs parts of the body that have a special job to do

pincers the pinching claws of an insect

predators animals that hunt and kill other animals

prey animals that are caught and eaten by other animals

raptors one of the main groups of birds of prey, with hooked beaks, strong feet, sharp talons, and large eyes

rodents the group of gnawing or nibbling mammals, such as rats and mice

scavenging feeding off dead animals

venom poison that is injected by some animals to attack their enemies

vibrations movements or sounds

Index

A
African wild ass 30
ambush 14, 17, 27
antivenin 15, 16

B
bactrian camels 12, 30
bilby 30
black-backed jackals 10–11

C
camels 12–13, 30
camouflage 9, 16, 26
carcass 11
colonies 8, 10, 18, 23
communication 19, 22, 26

D
dens 8
desert bandicoot 30
desert horned vipers 26–27
desert marsupial mouse 30
desert monitor lizard 30
desert plants 5
desert rat kangaroo 30
deserts 4
domestication 12–13
dromedary camels 12

E
echolocation 23
eggs 24–25
endangered animals 30

F
fangs 16, 26
fennec foxes 8–9
fighting 11, 13, 14, 19, 29
food chain 5
foxes 5, 8–9

G
ghost bats 22–23
gila monsters 14–15, 30
guard duty 18

H
habitat 5
Harris's hawks 20–21
hawks 5, 20–21
hearing 9, 22–23
herbivores 12–13
hibernation 15
hunting 6–7, 9–11, 14–15, 17, 19–21, 23, 27, 29

I
immunity 19
insect 5, 7

L
lizards 5, 14–15, 28–29, 30

M
meerkats 18–19
Mexican bobcat 30
monitor lizards 28–29, 30

N
nests 20

P
perenties 28–29
pincers 7

R
raptors 20–21
rat kangaroo 30
rats 5, 9

S
sand gazelle 30
scavenging 11, 29
scorpions 5, 6–7, 19
sight 19, 20
smell 19
snakes 5, 16–17, 26–27
spider-hunting wasps 24–25
survival 5

T
tails 6, 7, 9, 15, 28
tarantula hawk wasps 24–25
teeth 9, 13, 14, 16, 23, 26
temperature 4
tongues 9
tunnels 19

V
venom 6, 15, 16, 19, 24–25, 27
vibrations 6

W
water 9, 12–13
western diamondback rattlesnakes 16–17
World Wildlife Fund (WWF) 30